Go, Spud, Go!

adapted by Linda Estrella

based on the script by Ross Hastings

Ready-to-Read

Simon Spotlight

New York   London   Toronto   Sydney   Singapore

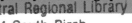

Based upon the television series *Bob the Builder*™
created by HIT Entertainment PLC and Keith Chapman,
as seen on Nick Jr.® Photos by HOT Animation.

SIMON SPOTLIGHT
An imprint of Simon & Schuster Children's Publishing Division
1230 Avenue of the Americas, New York, New York 10020
© 2004 HIT Entertainment PLC and Keith Chapman.
Manufactured in the United States of America
First Edition
2 4 6 8 10 9 7 5 3 1

Library of Congress Cataloging-in-Publication Data
Estrella, Linda.
Go, Spud, go! / adapted by Linda Estrella.—1st ed.
p. cm.—(Bob the Builder preschool ready-to-read ; 7)
"Based on the TV series Bob the Builder™ created by HIT
Entertainment PLC and Keith Chapman."
Summary: Spud has an accident because he is skateboarding too fast.
ISBN 0-689-86289-X (pbk.)
[1. Skateboarding—Fiction. 2. Potatoes—Fiction.] I. Chapman, Keith.
II. Title. III. Series: Bob the builder. Preschool ready-to-read ; 7.
PZ7.L9732Go 2004
[E]—dc21
2002156260

Spud has a skateboard!

Spud likes to go fast.

Go, Spud, go!

Uh-oh.

Look out, Spud!

Too fast, Spud!

Ouch!

Woof, woof, woof!
Scruffty wants to play.

Spud falls off his skateboard.

Poor Spud!

Bob is building a road.

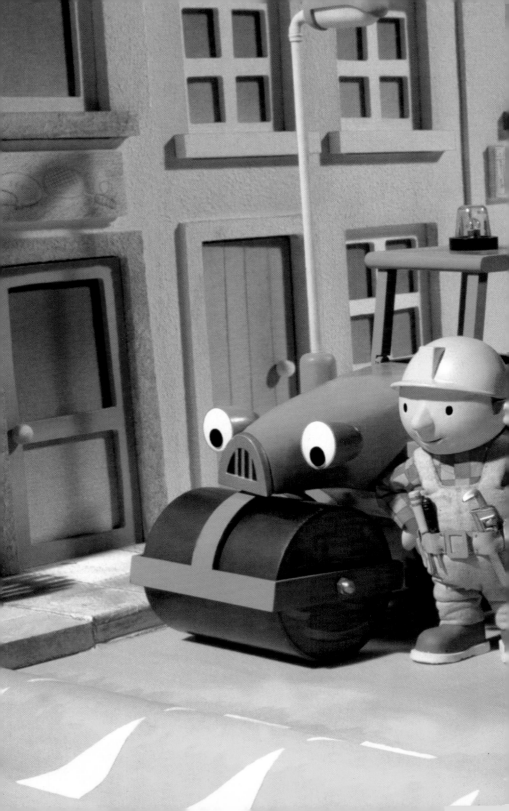

The road is done.

Good job, team!

Uh-oh.

Here comes Spud.

Spud skates fast.

Too fast!

Look out, Spud!

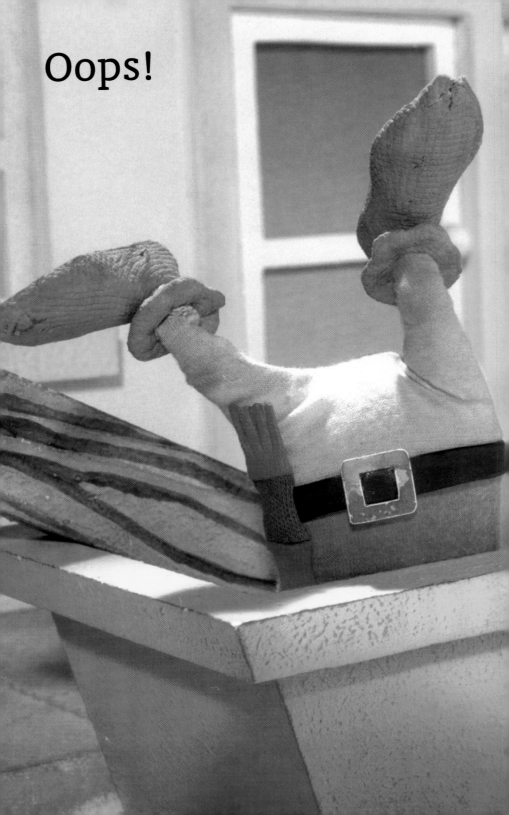

Oops!

Bob tries to help.

Poor Spud!